D0389334

GHOST DETECTORS
Pop!

BOOK 7

BY
DOTTI ENDERLE

ILLUSTRATED BY
HOWARD MCWILLIAM

magic
wagon

visit us at www.abdopublishing.com

A big thank you to Adrienne Enderle — DE
With thanks to my ever supportive wife Rebecca — HM

Published by Magic Wagon, a division of the ABDO Group,
8000 West 78th Street, Edina, Minnesota 55439. Copyright
© 2012 by Abdo Consulting Group, Inc. International copyrights
reserved in all countries. All rights reserved. No part of this
book may be reproduced in any form without written permission
from the publisher.

Calico Chapter Books™ is a trademark and logo of Magic Wagon.

Printed in the United States of America, Melrose Park, Illinois.
042011
092011
♻ This book contains at least 10% recycled materials.

Text by Dotti Enderle
Illustrations by Howard McWilliam
Edited by Stephanie Hedlund and Rochelle Baltzer
Cover and interior design by Jaime Martens

Library of Congress Cataloging-in-Publication Data

Enderle, Dotti, 1954-
  Pop! / by Dotti Enderle ; illustrated by Howard McWilliam.
     p. cm. -- (Ghost Detectors ; bk. 7)
  ISBN 978-1-61641-623-2 (alk. paper)
  [1. Chewing gum--Fiction. 2. Blessing and cursing--Fiction. 3.
Ghosts--Fiction. 4. Halloween--Fiction. 5. Humorous stories.] I.
McWilliam, Howard, 1977- ill. II. Title.
  PZ7.E69645Pop 2011
  [Fic]--dc22
                                   2011001231

Contents

Sitting Tight

"**W**hy is she always late?" Malcolm's best friend Dandy asked. "I'm hungry."

Dandy and Malcolm sat on the front porch steps waiting for Mail Carrier Nancy.

"She usually comes around one o'clock on Saturday," Malcolm reminded him. "It's only twelve thirty."

Dandy dug the toe of his sneaker between two of the boards on the porch

steps. It squeaked like a mouse playing a kazoo. "Why can't we eat lunch, then come out and wait for her?" he asked.

"You know why," Malcolm said. "I can't risk Cocoa getting that package before me. She'll hide it in her room somewhere and make me pay to get it back."

Dandy wiggled his toe in deeper. "I'm glad I don't have a sister."

"Yeah," Malcolm said. "It's a curse."

Malcolm checked up and down the sidewalk. He'd been waiting a whole month for this package, and he needed it by Halloween. Surely today would be his lucky day.

"How about I go and make us some sandwiches?" Dandy asked. "I could bring them out and we could have a porch picnic."

"It's not picnic weather," Malcolm reminded him. He pulled the collar of his jacket up around his neck. The October air had a biting chill. It was going to be an especially cold Halloween.

Dandy's jacket was about two sizes too big. When he pulled his collar up, his head disappeared. Malcolm unzipped it a little so Dandy could breathe.

"You look like a turtle," Malcolm said.

Dandy zipped it up again. "I'm not a turtle. Mail Carrier Nancy is. She's the slowpoke." He shoved his hands in his pockets and dug his toe deeper in between the squeaky boards.

Malcolm cringed. The only thing worse than that squeak was Cocoa practicing her choir solo. Her high notes could make your ears bleed.

"Would you stop that?" Malcolm said. "It's giving me chills."

"Are you sure it's me?" Dandy wondered. "I have chills too, but it's because it's freezing out here! My spit tastes like ice water."

More squeaking.

"Stop it, Dandy!"

"It's not me."

The noise grew louder. Just then, Mail Carrier Nancy turned the corner. She was dragging her squeaky mail cart behind her.

Cheep-cheep-cheep-cheep. Malcolm didn't mind that noise at all. He popped up off the porch and eagerly stood waiting for her.

Daddy hopped up, too. Almost. His sneaker was wedged tight between the

boards. *Splat!* He fell right onto the sidewalk.

"Are you okay?" Malcolm asked.

Dandy didn't answer. He just pointed back at his foot, jammed tight in the steps.

Malcolm reached over and grabbed Dandy's ankle. He braced himself and pulled . . . and tugged . . . and yanked . . . and *whoop!*

Dandy's foot popped free. But just his foot. His sneaker was still stuck in the steps.

"Dandy, are you okay?" Malcolm asked again, rolling his friend over. Malcolm expected to see scrapes and scratches and a bloody nose. But all he saw was . . . jacket. He unzipped it enough to uncover Dandy's face.

Dandy grinned. "This is why turtles never get bopped on the noggin." He zipped the jacket back up, burying his head.

Mail Carrier Nancy strolled up the sidewalk. "Here's your mail." She handed Malcolm a tall stack of envelopes of every shape and size.

"Thanks," he said, grabbing the stack.

Dandy was sitting back on the steps, playing tug-of-war with his sneaker. "Did it come?"

Malcolm shuffled through the stack.

There was a bright pink envelope for Cocoa. It smelled like the girly stores at the mall. Gag!

There were four envelopes for Grandma Eunice. Three were addressed to "Senior

Citizen," and one was a sample box of laxatives.

Malcolm's mom got an envelope full of super-saver coupons and an invitation to a bridal shower. Malcolm always wondered why the bride couldn't just take a bath like everyone else.

And there was an electric bill addressed to his dad. Poor Dad. All he ever got was bills.

Malcolm thumbed through each one, trying not to spill them on the ground. And just as he'd hoped, his envelope was on the bottom. It was crinkly and brown and sealed tight. "Yes!"

He was ready to rush in and open it, but Dandy was now swaying back and forth. He was dancing with that sneaker.

"It's crammed in tight," he told Malcolm.

"Just leave it, Dandy."

"I can't. These sneakers cost me about a year's worth of allowance. My dad'll kill me," Dandy moaned.

Malcolm surveyed the situation. "I think you're pulling the wrong direction. I'll grab one side, you grab the other. On the count of three pull back, okay?"

Daddy gripped one side and nodded.

"One . . . two . . . THREE!"

The sneaker popped loose, flew high into the air, and – *uh-oh* – landed on the roof.

Both boys stared up at the sneaker and blinked a few times.

"Just leave it," Dandy said, zipping his jacket up over his head.

X-Specs

Malcolm dropped the stack of mail on the hall table and hurried to his basement lab. Dandy stumbled along behind him.

"Open it," Dandy urged.

"Hang on. I don't want to just rip into it. This thing is delicate," Malcolm replied.

"No, I mean open my jacket. The zipper's stuck."

Malcolm helped Dandy out of his jacket, then he set his sights on the large envelope.

"This better be the X-ray glasses I ordered," he said.

Dandy leaned in, checking it out. "If you had them on, you could see right through it and tell if they were in there."

Malcolm rolled his eyes. "Or I could just open it."

He carefully dug his finger under the flap and ripped it loose. "Yes!" he shouted, pulling out a cellophane wrapper labeled:

Malcolm slipped the glasses from the cellophane and held them up to the light. They were round like goggles with red

and white swirls on the lenses. "These are perfect."

Dandy scratched his head, then his nose, then his head again. "But I don't get it. We can already see through ghosts. What do we need them for?"

"For Halloween," Malcolm said. "We can use these to x-ray our candy and make sure it's safe."

"My mom says I can only go to the houses of people I know. That's safe."

Malcolm tilted his head and gave Dandy a look. "Really? Last year we went to Nick Brunner's house. Remember what happened?"

Dandy scratched his nose again. "Oh, right. I still don't know how he got that garlic into our mini-Snickers without taking the wrappers off."

"Exactly," Malcolm said. "No one will trick us this year."

"Yeah," Dandy agreed. "We'll take the *trick* out of trick-or-treat."

Malcolm slipped the glasses on and everything went hazy.

"I can't see anything." Malcolm took a step back, staggering a little. "They make me kind of dizzy." He was about to take them off when he felt a small button on the side. The second he clicked it, the lenses began swirling round and round.

"Whoa!" Dandy said. "That's freaky."

Malcolm could barely see a thing. "What's happening?"

"It looks like your eyes are whirling in different directions. Can you see through me?"

Malcolm drooped. "I can't see anything but shadows." Had he wasted his money on a gag?

"Then will you take them off?" Dandy asked. "Those swirly whirlies make me want to take a nap."

Malcolm carefully looked around, hoping to see through walls. "They aren't working," he said.

"Maybe you're supposed to look at things up close," Dandy offered.

Malcolm put his hand up to his face. He could see his hand, but it looked fuzzy and blurred. "Hand me a flashlight."

Dandy did. Malcolm pressed the flashlight against his palm. Still blurry.

"Turn out the overhead light," he instructed.

Dandy switched it off.

His hand still looked blurry, but now it had a reddish glow, and . . . yes! He could see the veins inside. He jumped up and down.

"They work! They work!" Malcolm shouted. "I can see through my hand!"

Dandy eagerly grabbed the flashlight from Malcolm. "Let me try!" He pressed his palm to the light. "Look, Malcolm! I can see my veins, too! And I'm not even wearing the glasses!"

Malcolm slumped. Dandy was right. "I guess they don't work."

Dandy put them on. "They work great if you're trying not to see something."

He waved his hand in front of his face a few times then handed them back. Right then the basement door flew open and a voice screeched, "Malcolm!"

Cocoa clomped down the steps in her fleecy green bathrobe. She'd wrapped a towel on her head like a turban, and crammed big wads of cotton between her toes to keep from smearing her polish.

"It's your turn to rake the leaves!" she barked. "I did it last week!"

Malcolm quickly opened the glasses and slipped them back on.

Dandy cowered behind him and whispered, "I sure wish you'd bought an extra pair."

October 31

Ever since Malcolm ordered his Ecto-Handheld-Automatic-Heat-Sensitive-Laser-Enhanced Specter Detector, every day was Halloween. He just powered it up and *poof!* ghosts appeared before him.

But he wasn't thinking about ghosts tonight . . . not real ghosts anyway. He was thinking about candy.

Malcolm had come up with a perfect Halloween costume. First, he'd ripped up

one of his dad's old shirts and rolled it in dirt. Then he painted his face a smoky gray. He borrowed his mom's eyeliner to color his lips. Then he took Cocoa's black punk wig to top it all off.

"Feed me!" he growled, holding his arms out like a zombie.

Malcolm stayed in his room until the doorbell rang, and then rushed out to answer it. He wanted Dandy to be the first to see his great costume. He flung open the door and there stood . . . huh?

"Dandy, are you in there?"

Dandy was wrapped head to toe in white toilet paper. There was just one long open slit across the eyes so he could see. Malcolm guessed right away that he was a mummy, except . . .

"Dandy, why are you wearing green Spock ears?" Malcolm asked.

"Because I couldn't hear through all this tissue. I needed some help."

"But they're fake," Malcolm pointed out.

Dandy tilted a pointed ear toward him. "Huh?"

Malcolm shook his head. "Never mind."

"Going trick-or-treating?" a voice called from behind him. He turned just as Grandma Eunice wheeled into the room.

Malcolm gasped. She had a pirate's hat cocked on her head, lizard earrings dangling from her ears, and the X-Specs balancing on her nose.

"Grandma, what are you supposed to be?" Malcolm asked.

She pressed the button on the side of the X-Specs and the lenses circled round and round. She took off one of the lizard earrings and swung it back and forth.

"You are getting sleeeeepy," she droned. "Sleepier and sleepier."

"So you're a hypnotist?" Malcolm asked.

She kept swinging the lizard. "I'm going to hypnotize you and seize all your treasure."

"Is that why you're wearing a pirate's hat?"

"Arrrrrrr," she said, gritting her teeth.

"Hey, look what I can do," Dandy said, waddling closer. He took a deep breath

and poked his tongue through the toilet paper covering his mouth.

"That's a great trick," Grandma said.

Malcolm turned Dandy toward the door. "Let's go," he said.

Dandy spit out toilet paper as they grabbed their bags and left.

Malcolm and Dandy went to house after house after house. Malcolm couldn't believe how generous the neighbors were this year. His bag was nearly full by the time they'd made it to the next block.

"This is great!" he told Dandy. "Look at all this candy."

"Yeah," Dandy agreed. "And I got plenty of my favorite."

"What's your favorite?"

Dandy held up a handful. "Anything that ends with the word *pop*."

Malcolm nodded. "Can't go wrong there." He glanced up and down the street. "Should we go back or keep going?"

"Let's go home," Dandy said. "My backside is kind of cold."

Malcolm turned him around. "It's because a bunch of the toilet paper ripped off. I can sort of see your underwear."

"Do they show that much?"

"Dandy, they're red. Yes, they show."

"Oh, geez."

"Why did you wear red underwear under white toilet paper?"

Dandy shrugged. "Cause they match my socks."

"Let's just go."

When they got back to Malcolm's basement, Dandy ripped the toilet paper from his face. They both sat pretzel style on the floor.

"Let's dump it all in a big pile and divide it up," Malcolm said.

"Aren't we going to use the X-Specs?" Dandy asked.

Malcolm shook his head. "Those are only good for blocking out Cocoa."

With a mountain of candy in front of them, Malcolm began sorting it out. "We each get seven Fire Blasters, twelve Tangy Tarts, twenty Slimy Slurps —"

"Look!" Dandy interrupted. "Your grandma would like these." He held up some chocolate pirate coins.

"She can have them," Malcolm said. He continued counting. "Jelly beans,

jawbreakers, cinnamon and butterscotch wheels, and . . ."

"Bubble gum!" Dandy finished.

Malcolm arranged them by shape. Balls. Sticks. Nuggets. But there were a couple that really stood out.

"What are these?" Dandy asked. They looked like baseball card packets. The wrapper was black and silver with a large print on the front.

Dandy grabbed one. "Wow! I've never seen this kind before." When he ripped it open a long, gooey string of bubble gum oozed onto his lap. "And there's a card."

"What's on it?" Malcolm asked.

Dandy pulled the card from the wrapper and held it up. On one side was a photograph of a pudgy man wearing bright green suspenders, a pink bow tie, and a fez. He held a blob of gum in his open hands. On the other side, the caption read:

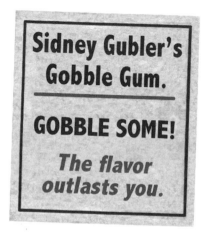

Sidney Gubler's Gobble Gum.

GOBBLE SOME!
The flavor outlasts you.

"Think this guy's Sidney Gubler?" Dandy asked.

"Probably," Malcolm said.

Dandy looked puzzled. "Why's he wearing a flowerpot on his head?"

"It's not a flowerpot. It's a fez."

Dandy looked even more puzzled—if that was possible. "Fuzz?"

"No, a fez," Malcolm corrected. "It's a type of hat."

Dandy nodded like he understood. "I bet if you pull that tassel on top a little monkey will pop out and do a dance."

"Dandy, if you pull that tassel on top, the fez will fall off his head."

"That would be funny, too," Dandy said.

"Just chew the gum."

"Well, okay then," Dandy crammed the whole mushy wad into his mouth.

Malcolm waited until Dandy had in a few good chews. "What's it taste like?"

"Cotton candy and whipped cream!" Dandy mumbled, gum drool dripping down his chin.

Malcolm opened his. The card had the same picture, but his said:

Sidney Gubler's Gobble Gum.

The flavor lasts a lifetime.

That was good enough for him. He popped the gum in his mouth.

Dandy was right. It was delicious! It was soft and easy to chew. Too easy. It felt like the gum was pulsing up and down between his teeth. It rolled from one side to the other just like a beach ball.

Weird. Maybe he should spit it out. But it tasted so good! Malcolm could chew this gum forever. But then he looked at the front of the wrapper. In small print were the words:

Hitching a Ride

After Dandy left, Malcolm headed toward his room. But just as he reached the door —*"Aaaaaah!"*— the freakiest, hairiest, most terrifying witch ever blocked his way. She pinned him to the wall with her broom.

"I didn't get any super chocolate fantasy bars, and I bet you did. Hand one over," Cocoa demanded.

Malcolm reached up and thumped the rubber wart off his sister's nose. "Why

should I share with you? You never give me anything," Malcolm replied.

Cocoa raised the broom up over his head. "I'll give you something now if you don't hand over a fantasy bar."

"Why don't you just hop on that thing and fly away," Malcolm suggested.

"I've got a better idea." Cocoa came down hard with the broom and whacked

Malcolm on the head. The black punk wig slid off and plopped on the floor.

Cocoa looked down. "Hey! Is that my wig? You little creep!"

When she bent down to pick it up, Malcolm pushed her out of the way and made a dash for his room. Just before going in he dropped a fantasy bar on the floor.

That should keep her from ripping the door off, he thought.

Malcolm wiped off the last of his zombie face and got ready for bed. The gum still worked its way around his mouth. He did some homework, read for a while, then turned out the light.

He had planned to spit the gum in the trash, but it still hadn't lost its flavor. In fact, the more he chewed, the more flavorful it got. But it was late and he needed to sleep.

Malcolm tore out a piece of notebook paper, wrapped the gum inside, and put it on his desk. Then, he crawled back into bed. It wasn't long before he drifted into dreamland.

In his dreams, Malcolm was still chewing the gum. It was delicious! He chewed the gum all the time. He even brushed his teeth with it! And not only that, he passed out stacks and stacks to his classmates and became the school hero.

In the dream, Malcolm won first place in the science fair, won the grand prize in the talent show, and was voted class president. When he got up to make his acceptance speech, he was still chewing the gum. And so was everyone else.

His dreams were so amazing, Malcolm didn't want to wake up. But his alarm went

buzzzzzz and he was jerked back into reality. Same old Malcolm. Same old thing.

Malcolm scratched his head, stretched, then yawned. *Huh?* Malcolm worked his jaw. Something was definitely inside his mouth. He chewed. The gum! It was back in his mouth.

The piece of notebook paper he'd wrapped it in was crumpled on the floor. That made no sense. How did the gum get back in his mouth? *Sleepwalking.* That had to be it. How else? His dreams had been so good, he got up in the night, reached for the gum, and popped it back in.

Malcolm chewed the gum while he got ready for school. He took it out long enough to eat a bowl of cereal and brush his teeth. Then he chewed some more until it was time to head out to the bus stop.

He couldn't believe that it had survived hours of chewing and still tasted so good. He wrapped it in some more notebook paper and left it on his night table. It'd be there when he got home.

Malcolm plopped down next to Dandy on the bus. "I think the day after Halloween should be an official holiday," he said. "No fair that we have to go to school after trick-or-treating."

"I know," Dandy mumbled. Malcolm sort of heard what Dandy said, but it came out kind of garbled. "Are you chewing gum?" he asked.

Dandy clapped his hand over his mouth. "Yeah. But don't tell anyone. I'll get in trouble."

"You can't chew gum at school."

"I know," Dandy whispered. "It just tasted too good to spit out."

"That is some great gum," Malcolm agreed. "But you're really risking it. If Mrs. Goolsby catches you, you'll get detention."

Dandy nodded. "I'll take it out before school starts."

When they got to their classroom, Malcolm put his backpack down on his desk. He pulled out his textbooks, a pencil, last night's homework, and . . . what?

Right next to his lunch was a wadded piece of notebook paper. Malcolm froze. His heart thumped like a paddleball as he carefully took out the paper. He recognized it. It was the same paper he'd used to wrap the gum—the gum he'd left at home!

Malcolm slowly pulled it open, and there it was! Only now it was the size of a ping-pong ball, and it was pulsating.

It's Back!

Yikes! Malcolm hurried over to the trash can and tossed the gum in. How could the gum have hitched a ride in his backpack?

He glanced back. Dandy's jaw worked up and down in a rhythm. Why hadn't Dandy spit out his gum? Was he chewing it because he wanted to, or because he had to? Malcolm wasn't sure!

"Take your places, everyone," Mrs. Goolsby said as she wrote a word problem

on the board. *Ugh.* He had bigger problems than math. But then he read the problem.

Sally bought 3 packs of bubble gum and 1 pack of chewing gum. She paid $1.75. Jim bought 2 packs of bubble gum and 4 packs of chewing gum. He paid $2.00. Find the cost of a pack of bubble gum and the cost of a pack of chewing gum.

Malcolm looked over at Dandy. Dandy's eyes were bugged out and a little gum juice was dribbling down his chin.

This had to be a coincidence. Why did Mrs. Goolsby decide to use that math problem?

Malcolm scribbled it down on a piece of paper and went to work. Only he couldn't concentrate. His eyes kept drifting over to the trash can. Was the gum still pulsing in there?

Malcolm went back to work on the problem. The word *gum* kept jumping off the page, disappearing, then coming back. He didn't know how much Sally paid for a pack of gum. He didn't care. Why couldn't Mrs. Goolsby have used a different example? Maybe some chocolate nuggets or cinnamon doodles?

The room was filled with the *scritch-scratch* of pencils. That should've been the only noise. But there was one other. A juicy *Smack! Smack! Smack!*

Malcolm took a quick peek. Dandy was chewing, but he was too far away to be heard. What was it? *Smack! Smack! Smack!* Where was it coming from?

Then Malcolm saw it coming toward him. It pushed in and out like a slimy slug slowly crossing his desk. *Smack! Smack! Smack!*

"Ahhhhhhhh!" Malcolm screamed, stabbing the gum with his pencil. It wiggled and squirmed, trying to break free.

"Gum!" Mrs. Goolsby barked. "You brought gum to school?"

"It's not mine," Malcolm said. Which was true. Malcolm had thrown it away, so it really wasn't his anymore.

Mrs. Goolsby pointed to the trash can. "Get rid of it."

Malcolm rose, holding the pencil away from him. He might as well have speared a snake. Since he wasn't about to touch that gum, he leaned over and tossed it in, pencil and all.

"Now back to work," Mrs. Goolsby ordered.

Malcolm grabbed a fresh pencil and went back to the problem. But he couldn't shake the jitters.

When lunchtime came, Malcolm relaxed. He'd made it through the morning and even solved that gum-filled math problem. He and Dandy settled at their usual table.

"I can't believe you're still chewing that gum," Malcolm said. "It's got to taste like rubber by now."

Dandy shook his head. "The label was right. The flavor does last a lifetime."

"Well, you certainly won't if Mrs. Goolsby catches you."

"That's what's weird," Dandy said. "When she looks over at me, the gum stops chewing."

"What do you mean, it 'stops chewing'?" Malcolm asked.

"It crawls up to the roof of my mouth and flattens out. Then when she turns around, it starts chewing again."

"Dandy, the gum doesn't chew, you do," Malcolm said.

"Not this gum. It can do jumping jacks in my mouth. All by itself."

"Jumping jacks? That's crazy. You're going to have to take it out to eat lunch."

"I can't," Dandy said. "It just plastered itself on the top of my mouth again."

"Whatever."

Malcolm opened his lunch sack and dumped his food on the table. Today he had a peanut butter and jelly sandwich, an apple, and a juice box. He was starving.

Malcolm unwrapped his sandwich and took a huge bite. *Mmmm,* this was the best sandwich he'd ever eaten. He swallowed the bread, but noticed that a glob of peanut butter was still stuck in his mouth.

He rolled the blob around, chomping and chewing. He tried to swallow, but it wouldn't go down. He chomped and chewed some more.

Every time he gulped, the peanut butter clung to his teeth. He tried spitting it out,

but it crawled down and burrowed in his cheek.

"What's wrong?" Dandy asked. "Are you choking? Should I call the nurse or something?"

Malcolm desperately clawed at the gob in his mouth. He finally grabbed it, pulled it out, and . . . no! He was holding the bubble gum, and it had gotten even larger!

Double Gum

Malcolm dropped the gum on the table and beat it with his fist.

"You didn't tell me that you'd brought more gum," Dandy said.

"I didn't bring it, Dandy. It hitchhiked," Malcolm replied.

Dandy laughed a little. "Well, how could it do that? It doesn't have any thumbs."

"I'm telling you," Malcolm said. "I didn't bring it. It's following me somehow."

"What're you going to do?"

Malcolm wondered that, too. "What do you think I should do?" he asked.

Dandy smacked his gum a few times. "I think you should just put it back in your mouth and chew it."

"I don't want to chew it."

Dandy smacked a few more times. "But it's delicious."

"I know, but if we're only chewing gum all the time we'll starve."

Dandy stopped smacking. He dug two fingers into his mouth, pinching at the gum. He wiggled and squirmed and gagged a few times.

"I can't grab it. It's too fast for me." His eyes bugged in panic.

"Don't worry," Malcolm assured him. "We'll get it out."

Dandy opened his mouth so wide Malcolm could see his tonsils. "Can you catch it?" he asked.

Malcolm blanched. "Uh . . . we're best friends and all, but I'm not sticking my fingers in your mouth."

"I'd do it for you," Dandy said.

That's true. Dandy would do whatever it'd take to help Malcolm out. "I've got an idea," he said.

Malcolm walked around the table, stood behind Dandy, then *whack!* He slapped Dandy on the back as hard as he could.

Dandy's cheeks puffed and the gum went shooting out. It bulleted across the cafeteria and landed in a pile of peas on Milton Freebok's tray. (Which was okay since Milton only ate the meatballs, never the peas.)

"This is crazy," Malcolm said. "Something's wrong with that gum."

Dandy rubbed his jaws. "Maybe it's made out of rubber."

"It doesn't bounce," Malcolm said.

Dandy rubbed his cheeks. "Maybe it's made out of paste."

Malcolm thought about that. "No. Our mouths would've been glued shut."

They both looked down at Malcolm's gum still lying on the table. It pulsed, throbbed, and thumped. A chill ran down Malcolm's spine.

"Maybe it's alive!" he said. He speared the gum with the straw from his juice box and crammed it inside his lunch sack. "Take that!" he said, wadding it up in a tight ball.

They glanced over at Dandy's gum. It looked like a lumpy pink eraser lying on a pile of green mush. (Milton didn't eat the peas, but he liked to mash them up.)

"We've got to do something," Malcolm said. "If there's any more gum out there like this, it could take over the world."

"Yeah," Dandy agreed. "Everyone could become gum zombies."

Malcolm looked down at the crumpled sack in his hands. "I don't want to become a gum zombie."

"Me either," Dandy said. "What are we going to do?"

"Do you remember who gave us this gum? Which house it was?"

Dandy shrugged. "How should I know? I was squinting through a wrapping of two-ply."

Some Serious Snooping

After school, Malcolm waited for Dandy on the corner. There were three things he knew for sure: It was November 1, it was cold, and he had to rid the world of zombie gum.

Pretty soon, Malcolm saw an enormous jacket strolling up. He knew Dandy was somewhere inside it.

"You ready to do this?" Malcolm asked.

Dandy unzipped the jacket and poked his head out. "Let's make it quick. I feel like a freezer pop."

Malcolm pointed the way. "It's two streets over."

When they reached the intersection, Dandy pointed to the street sign. Malcolm looked up. They were at the corner of Sweet Gum Lane and Swell Street.

"I should've remembered," Dandy said.

Malcolm turned onto Sweet Gum. "It's down here."

The wind had picked up and leaves swirled around their feet. A cloud covered the sun, turning the sky a ghostly gray. They continued on. Their target was four houses down on the right.

"You think we should do this?" Dandy asked through chattering teeth.

"Why? Are you scared?" Malcolm asked.

Dandy zipped his jacket up over his head. "No. I'm just cold."

Malcolm was shivering too, but the weather had little to do with it. "This won't take long," he assured Dandy. Or was he really assuring himself?

The doorbell went *ding*, then stuck. The door creaked open and a woman appeared. She was as round as she was tall. Her snow-white hair was feathered. And her teeth were as fake as Cocoa's punk wig. With a beaming grin she said, "Are you selling Boy Scout cookies?"

Malcolm shuffled his feet. "No, ma'am. Boy Scouts don't sell cookies."

She placed a hand to her cheek. "No Boy Scout cookies?"

Malcolm took a deep breath. "There are no Boy Scout cookies. Just Girl Scout cookies."

"Oh. Then I'll take two boxes!"

Malcolm looked at Dandy. Dandy shrugged. "No, ma'am. We're not selling Girl Scout cookies either."

"What a shame," she said, folding her arms. "Are you selling peanut brittle?"

Malcolm clenched his fists and drew in a breath. *Stay calm,* he told himself. "We're not selling anything. We're here to ask about your Halloween candy," he said.

The woman placed her hands on her hips and glared at them. "Why, you little beggars. Didn't you get enough last night?"

"Yes," Malcolm said. "It's just that the gum you gave us was so good we're wondering where you got it."

The woman's face grew pale. "Oh dear. What did it look like?"

"It had a black wrapper with a mouth on the front," Malcolm said.

The woman clutched her heart. "It must have gotten mixed up with the other candy somehow." She leaned against the doorjamb. "Oh my. There were only two pieces left. I had it hidden away."

"It ended up in our treat bags," Dandy said.

"Whatever you do, don't chew it!" she warned. "My late husband, Freddy, brought that gum back from his trip to Greater Tasmundo. I couldn't chew any because of my dentures. But he did." A tear slid down her cheek. "And the gum chewed him up."

Malcolm felt his knees go weak. "Chewed him up?"

The woman clutched his arm. "Yes. Whatever you do, don't chew that gum!"

Malcolm nodded, not wanting her to know it was too late. "Okay. Thanks."

When she closed the door, Malcolm turned around. "Dandy? Dandy? Where are you?" That's when he saw the huge bulky jacket frantically running away.

The Blob

Back at the basement lab, Malcolm tried to calm Dandy down. He looked like he'd seen a ghost. No, worse. Dandy had seen lots of ghosts and none of them had scared him like this.

"Malcolm . . . I - I - I - I don't want to get chewed up," Dandy stuttered.

"You're not going to get chewed up. Remember, we tossed the gum at lunch today. It's gone," Malcolm reminded him.

"But what if it comes back?" Dandy whimpered.

Malcolm patted Dandy's shoulder. "It probably won't." Though deep down, he wasn't so sure. "Here." He dumped his treat bag on the floor. An assortment of chocolate bars, suckers, and jelly beans spilled out. "There's no school tomorrow. We have no homework. And you're sleeping over tonight. Let's celebrate with some candy."

They each grabbed a chocolate bell and unwrapped it. Dandy popped his into his mouth. But Malcolm paused. "D-Dandy," he said, "does this look familiar to you?"

"Oh geez!" Dandy shouted.

Malcolm had unwrapped his, but it wasn't chocolate inside. It was the gum!

"Ahhhhh!" Malcolm scootched back, kicking it across the floor.

Dandy froze for a moment, then reached into his mouth, clawing at the piece he was chewing. "Rum Rubby! Rum Rubby!"

"Get your hand out of your mouth, Dandy. I can't understand you."

Dandy dropped his hand and shouted, "Gum zombie! I'm going to become a gum zombie!"

"Don't worry. I'll get it out for you." Malcolm hopped up and dug through his tools, scattering some on the floor. He grabbed the pliers. "This should work." But just as he took a step back, he felt something wormy and wet crawling up his leg. "No!"

Malcolm twisted and kicked, trying to shake it loose. The gum moved faster and

faster. He wiggled and jerked. Soon it was creeping across his belly.

Malcolm tugged at his shirt, but the gum was too quick. He grabbed at it as it inched up his neck. The gum dodged. Then suddenly, it disappeared. Malcolm couldn't feel it at all. He spun in circles, searching front and back. It was gone.

"You sticky little leech. Where are you?" He turned Dandy. "Where is it?"

But Dandy had his own problems. He had blown a bubble about the size of his head, and was wrestling on the floor with it.

Malcolm grabbed a ballpoint pen and— *POP!*—the gum exploded backward and covered Dandy's face.

"Thanks," Dandy said, huffing and puffing. "I couldn't breathe." Dandy

picked at his gum mask, trying to pull it off. But bits and pieces kept sticking to his fingers.

Malcolm spread his arms and legs. "I can't find my gum. Do you see it anywhere?"

"Uh-oh." Dandy's gaze rose higher and higher. "Malcolm, you have gum in your hair."

Malcolm stepped over to his work desk and grabbed the toaster he'd used to make the Super Toss, a Frisbee thrower that had once helped save their lives at a campsite. He checked his reflection in it. The image was squished and warped, but he could see it. The gum sat right on the top of his head. It stood straight up like a pink pointing finger.

Malcolm set the toaster down slowly. No sudden moves. He pretended to scratch his ear. Then his nose. Then his forehead. Then *snap!* Like a flash he reached up and grabbed the gum. "Ouch!" It was stuck in his hair.

"Dandy, help!"

"I can't." Dandy was lying on the floor. The thin layer of gum covering his face was blowing a gazillion tiny bubbles all over. Dandy hit at them like someone playing Whack-A-Mole at a carnival.

Malcolm dashed over. "I'll get this off y—" He never completed the sentence. Once his mouth was open, the gum in his hair did a swan dive onto his nose, then tucked and curled and bounced right into his mouth.

"We're going to turn into gum zombies!" Dandy cried.

And for the first time, Malcolm believed it.

Sidney's Revenge

Malcolm spit and sputtered. He bit down hard, hoping to smoosh it. But the gum grew and grew and grew. It forced his mouth open, then expanded into a huge balloon-like bubble.

He waited until it stretched so thin he could see right through it. Then *jab!* He stabbed it with a ballpoint pen. It exploded backward, covering Malcolm from head to toe. He felt like a pork chop wrapped in pink cellophane.

Malcolm struggled with his wrapping, bending and stretching. He finally managed to tear a hole by his ear and pull it off of his face. He was having better luck than Dandy, who was completely cocooned in the gum. Dandy lay curled on the floor with his knees up to his chin. The perfect gum ball.

"I'll save you, Dandy!"

Malcolm struggled forward, but he might as well have been on the surface of the moon. Each step was in slow motion.

He'd nearly reached Dandy when he noticed something strange. (Yes, even stranger than being attacked by giant blobs of killer gum.) Long threads of the gum were reaching up and out like marionette strings, and something was controlling it! And Malcolm had a pretty good idea what it was.

"Hang in there, Dandy!"

"Wuwwy!" Dandy said through the gum.

Malcolm tried to hurry, but he could barely move his foot. He pulled and pulled.

"Wuwwy!" Dandy urged again.

"I'm trying, but there's gum stuck to my shoe!"

Malcolm wiggled his foot, trying to scrape it off. "Ew!"

He managed to trudge forward, shuffling through the elastic gunk. He finally reached his desk. Right there next to his X-Specs, lay his Ecto-Handheld-Automatic-Heat-Sensitive-Laser-Enhanced Specter Detector. Malcolm powered it up and switched it on.

Usually ghosts just magically appear when the specter detector does its job. Not this time. This ghost wavered in and out like vapor from a fog machine. But finally Malcolm could see him from head to toe. And he recognized him right away.

"You!" Malcolm shouted. "You're Sidney Gubler. The guy on the bubble gum card. Uh . . . you're the ghost?"

"Well, of course," Sidney smirked. "You didn't really think there was such a thing as cursed bubble gum, did you?"

Actually, Malcolm had. He carefully reached behind him for his ghost zapper.

"Why?" Malcolm asked, trying to buy some time. Who knew how long the ghost would wait.

"Why'd I do it?" the ghost said. "Because I devoted my life to perfecting the most

delicious bubble gum the world could ever imagine. Gum that was so flavorful that people would rather chew it than bicker or fight. How could anyone be angry when their mouth is full of sweet bursts of crystal? It was the perfect plan. I should've won the Nobel Peace Prize!"

Sidney hung his head. "But my dreams were shattered," he went on. "Destroyed."

Malcolm continued to reach for the ghost zapper. Slowly . . . slowly . . .

"Everyone in Greater Tasmundo loved my gum," Sidney explained. "They chewed it constantly. And because of it, people were always nice and polite. They said please and thank you and opened doors for each other. It was glorious! But then, everything came crashing down."

Malcolm could feel the zapper. He had to keep the ghost talking. "Why?"

The ghost said, "Linda Lou Tweezle. She loved the gum, chewed it all the time. But one day she coughed. When she did the gum flew out of her mouth, made a perfect arc, and dropped straight down into Dirk Fender's throat.

"Dirk was looking up, balancing a ball on his nose at the time. He was always a show-off. Anyway, the gum stuck right in his gullet. He choked and choked and you can only imagine what happened next."

Malcolm shrugged a little. "What?"

"Instead of spitting the gum out, he swallowed it. And you know what they say about swallowing gum." Sidney lowered his voice like he was sharing a secret. "It makes your stomach stick together."

Malcolm didn't know if that was true, but he had heard it before.

"After that, no one would chew my gum. They said it was deadly and dangerous." He sighed. "I wasn't a hero after all, and I didn't win the Nobel Prize. So I swore that after my death, I would use my gum for evil instead of good."

"Well, that's just stupid," Malcolm said, finally gripping the ghost zapper. He lightly tapped it on.

"Is it?" he said with an evil grin. "We'll see who's stupid."

He pointed his finger at Dandy. The gum crissed and crossed, tying a large gummy bow on top of Dandy's head.

Dandy gave Malcolm a panicked look. "Eek! Eek!" Malcolm knew that he was really yelling, "Help! Help!" He swung the ghost zapper up, aimed, and . . .

Just before he pulled the trigger, the ghost went *pop!* and disappeared.

A Mesmerizing Outcome

Malcolm did a full circle, looking around.

"Where wee woe?" Dandy mumbled.

"I don't know," Malcolm said, "but I don't think he's gone for good."

"Wit me wout ah here!"

Malcolm tramped forward. It felt like he was dancing in sludge. He knelt and peeled the gum off Dandy's face.

Dandy panted for air. Then his eyes drifted up just above Malcolm's head.

"Uh . . . Malcolm . . ."

Malcolm waited just a beat, then he whipped around, looking the ghost straight in the face. He raised the ghost zapper then *pop!* the sly ghost vanished again.

"Come out!" Malcolm yelled. He held the zapper out, twisting this way and that, just like the detectives on his favorite crime show.

Dandy managed to pull loose from his gum trap. He stood behind Malcolm, ready for action. They crept back-to-back around the basement lab.

"You think he's gone for good?" Dandy asked.

Just then, a sticky wad of gum dropped onto Malcolm's shoulder. "Ew!" He raised

the zapper up. Sidney was hanging from the ceiling.

"Miss me?" the ghost teased.

Malcolm pulled the trigger, but the electric rays of the zapper just bounced away. Sidney got away again.

"We've got to find a way to trap him," Malcolm said. Then he saw the solution. There on his desk were the X-Specs!

He fumbled a bit, but managed to put them on and flip the switch. The lenses swirled round and round.

"Take those off," Dandy said. "You won't be able to see the ghost."

"No, but you will." He motioned for Dandy to look around the lab. "Let me know when you see him."

"Okay," Dandy said. "But this makes no sense."

"It makes perfect sen—"

"In the corner!" Dandy shouted, turning Malcolm in that direction.

"What's that on your face?" the ghost asked. But that was the last thing he said. He stared straight at the churning circles of the X-Specs . . . and froze.

"You hypnotized him," Dandy whispered.

"Yeah. And now I'm going to vaporize him." Malcolm held up the zapper, took aim and *zap!* Gone for good.

Malcolm took off the specs and grinned. "Guess we burst his bubble." He held up his palm, and Dandy slapped him five. But then their hands stuck together from all the gum.

"How are we going to get all this gum off?" Dandy asked, picking at the icky mess.

"I heard you rub peanut butter on it," Malcolm answered.

Dandy picked some off his nose. "I heard you're supposed to use mayonnaise."

Malcolm shrugged. "Let's use both." They slogged up the stairs to the kitchen.

That afternoon, Malcolm and Dandy sat on the porch. Malcolm had his treat bag on his lap. He dug in, pulling out all the gum he'd gotten Halloween night. "I'm never chewing another piece of gum for the rest of my life!"

"Me either," Dandy said. "I'm sticking to chocolate bars and butterscotch. But do you think it's safe to throw that away? What if it comes back?"

Malcolm hadn't thought of that. Would it come back? Is any gum safe now?

Right then, Cocoa came storming out the door. "Hey, goofus!" she howled. "You haven't raked the leaves yet. I'm going to tell Mom."

"Wow, Cocoa, are you still dressed for Halloween?" Malcolm asked, pointing at her orange and gold plaid shirt with silver fringe. "'Cause you look like a disco scarecrow."

"Yeah," Dandy agreed. "A disco scarecrow."

Cocoa stood with her fists on her hips. Malcolm thought smoke might curl from her nostrils at any minute. "That's it! I'm telling Mom."

"Fine," Malcolm said. "Then I'm not going to share my gum with you."

Cocoa looked down and her eyes lit like spotlights. "Is that Purple Yum Gum?"

"Yeah," Malcolm said, offering her some. "As a matter of fact, you can have all of it."

She looked suspicious. "You still have to rake the yard, bird brain."

"Okay, okay. I'll rake the yard."

Cocoa scooped up the gum and hurried back inside.

"I know she's screwy," Dandy said. "But she is your sister. Do you think that was safe?"

"Are you kidding?" Malcolm said. "Once Cocoa starts chomping, that gum won't have a chance." He held out the candy. "Now, which one do you want? Chocolate or butterscotch?"

Dandy grinned. "Both!"

TOOLS OF THE TRADE: FIVE USES FOR X-SPECS

From Ghost Detectors Malcolm and Dandy

X-Specs are useful tools for a ghost detector. Here are five things you can do with your X-Specs:

1. Entertain your grandma with an afternoon of pirate hypnosis.

2. Make yourself and your friends dizzy.

3. Freeze a spirit in its tracks so you can zap it with your Ecto-Handheld-Automatic-Heat-Sensitive-Laser-Enhanced Ghost Zapper.

4. Keep your ghost dog entertained while you do your homework.

5. Avoid seeing your sister stomping toward you!